CAPTAIN CAT
AND THE TREASURE MAP!

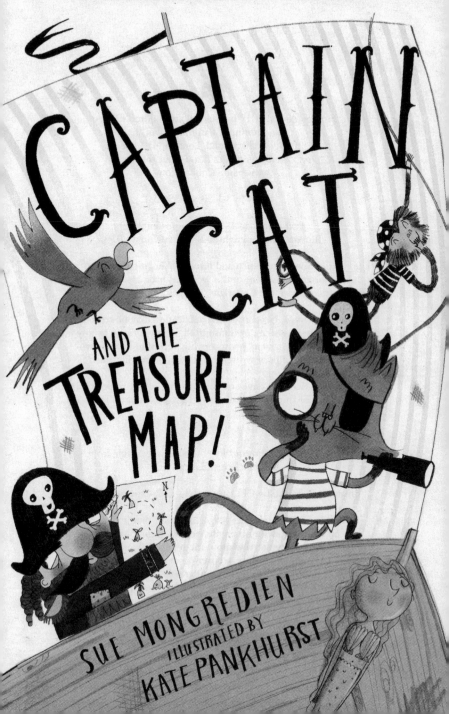

CAPTAIN CAT

AND THE TREASURE MAP!

SUE MONGREDIEN

ILLUSTRATED BY

KATE PANKHURST

First published 2019 by Macmillan Children's Books
an imprint of Pan Macmillan
20 New Wharf Road, London N1 9RR
Associated companies throughout the world
www.panmacmillan.com

ISBN 978-1-5098-8390-5

1 3 5 7 9 8 6 4 2

A CIP catalogue record for this book is available from
the British Library.

Printed and bound by CPI Group (UK) Ltd, Croydon CR0 4YY

This book belongs to:

THE CREW OF THE

PATCH

CUTLASS

CANNONBALL

CAPTAIN HALIBUT

Chapter One

It was a sunny morning on board the *Golden Earring* and Patch the pirate puss was patrolling the ship, sniffing the salty sea air.

There was Cutlass the green pirate parrot, thinking up brilliant new jokes.

There was Monty the annoying ship's monkey, picking his fleas and eating bananas.

And there was Captain Halibut, working hard as usual . . . Oh. Wait, no, he wasn't. He was putting his foot up and snoozing in a deckchair.

Patch gave her claws a sneaky sharpening on

the mast while he wasn't looking.

'Tum-te-tum,' she hummed under her breath.

Around the other side of the ship, a

disgusting stink

wafted out from the galley kitchen where the ship's cook, Cannonball, was making his famous tentacle stew. Famously BAD, that is. Patch hurried quickly through the pong, eyes watering. *Yuck.*

An even more revolting smell wafted out from the ship's toilet where Butch . . . well, actually, let's not go into details about what Butch was doing.

'Pooh,' muttered Patch, wrinkling her nose and walking even faster.

Exactly.

Meanwhile, Ginger was in the crow's nest. She was the only pirate brave enough to climb all the way up there. 'Eleven o'clock and all's well, me hearties,' she called down.

Arrrr, this is the life, thought Patch, settling down in a warm spot of sunshine for a cosy cat-nap. The ship was peaceful. Everything was calm. Shush . . . *shush* . . . sighed the sea against the sides of the ship and, for once, even the screeching seagulls fell silent.

Then the trouble started.

BANG! went the kitchen door, swinging open as Cannonball staggered out. He was carrying an enormous pot, piled so high with potatoes that he couldn't see over the top of them.

'Ginger!' he yelled. 'Where is she? Ginger, I've got a job for you!'

'Ahoy!' Ginger replied cheerfully, scrambling down the rigging. 'On my way, Cannonball.'

Patch opened her one green eye and spied Monty, who was chortling naughtily as he chucked a banana skin in front of the cook.

'Uh-oh!' she cried, jumping up at once. But she was too late.

Cannonball stepped on the banana skin and his feet skidded out from under him. *Wheeeeee!* 'Whoooaaa!' he shouted.

THUMP!

'*Oof!*' went the cook, landing splat on his back.

CLANG! went the pot as it dropped from his hands.

THUD **THUD** THUD THUD THUDDETY THUD went the potatoes rolling and bowling all over the deck.

5

As the wave of spuds thundered straight at her,

Patch leapt out the way, her paws outstretched.

'Meooow!' she cried in alarm.

6

'Watch out!' squawked Cutlass.

'Wahhhh!' yelped Ginger, swerving to dodge the flying cat. But she swerved a bit too far, and . . .

SPLOSH! Ginger plunged headfirst into the sea, splattering the snoozing captain with cold, salty water.

'What the . . . ?' spluttered Captain Halibut, falling out of his deckchair.

'HELP!' wailed Ginger from the water, arms flailing.

'PIRATE OVERBOARD!' screeched Cutlass, flying around in circles. 'GINGER OVERBOARD!'

Unfortunately, none of the pirates understood parrot language. They didn't speak cat or monkey either. While this meant that Patch, Cutlass and Monty could say anything they liked about the crew without them knowing, it also meant that sometimes – like now! – it wasn't very easy to alert the pirates to danger.

Hearing the racket, Butch charged out from the toilet, still pulling up his pants.

'NOBODY PANIC!' he bellowed. But then he saw his shipmate struggling in the sea and clapped his hands to his face. 'HELP! SHE'S GOING TO DROWN!' he shrieked.

Cannonball sat up and rubbed his round, shiny head. 'My potatoes . . .' he moaned.

'Devil's dogfish,' growled Captain Halibut, stamping to the side of the ship. *Stamp*-*clonk*, *stamp*-*clonk* went the sound of his wooden leg.

'What's all the rumpus?'

'I'm . . . *blub-blub-blub* . . . sinking!' gulped Ginger, thrashing about below.

Honestly, thought Patch, strolling across the deck towards a large coil of rope. *Sometimes pirates are soooo useless!* She shoved at the rope with her paws, sending one end snaking over the side of the ship.

'Ahoy, Cutlass!' she yelled, and the parrot flapped across the ship, grabbed the rope in his beak and swooped down with it to Ginger.

Then he fluttered back to high-five Patch, claw to paw.

Patch smiled. 'Easy-peasy!'

'Heave! Heave! Heave!' grunted Butch, doing his best to haul Ginger out of the sea.

'*Coo-ee!* Let me help!' came a voice. Patch peered overboard to see a mermaid who'd just popped up in the sea nearby.

'**Hurrrggh-ha!**' And with her mighty mermaid muscles she gave Ginger a powerful push.

'**Whoaaa!**' yelled Ginger, flying through the air. She fell onto the deck, dripping wet and puffing like a puffer fish. 'Phew. Thanks, Shelly!' she called to the friendly mermaid, who gave her a cheerful wave in return. Then Ginger shook herself dry, sneezed some seaweed out of her nose and held up a green glass bottle with a cork in one end.

'Guys, look what I found,' she said with a watery grin.

'Is it rum?' asked Cannonball hopefully.

Ginger yanked out the cork with her teeth and peered into the bottle.

'There's some paper inside,' she said, pulling it out carefully. 'Ooh!' she exclaimed, dropping the bottle as she unrolled a weathered old scroll. 'It's a map!'

Patch pricked up her ears at Ginger's excited voice. *A map? Cool!*

Ginger peered at the parchment, scratching her head. 'Cuh-cuh-CUSTARD, tuh-tuh-TREATS map!' she spelled out, then beamed. 'Oh yay, I love custard!'

Cutlass landed on a nearby cannon. 'I say, I say, I say: what's yellow and stupid?' he squawked to Patch.

'I know what's *green* and stupid,' called Monty nastily, dangling upside down from the rigging and

Hey, Cap'n, what's yellow and stupid?

showing everyone his horrid pink monkey bottom.

The other two ignored him.

'*Thick* custard,' Cutlass laughed to Patch. 'Get it, matey? **Thick** custard!'

Captain Halibut snatched the map from Ginger.

'I'll have that,' he snapped, then gave one of his legendary nostril-quivering snorts as he read the map. 'It doesn't say ***custard treats***, you deep-sea dimwit, it says ***cursed treasure***!'

'Talking of thick . . .' Patch whispered to Cutlass.

Thick custard

13

'Whoops,' said Ginger, looking disappointed. 'I fancied a custard treat.'

Captain Halibut did *not* look disappointed. His moustache was practically waggling with joy. 'Who cares about custard when this is a *treasure* map?' he cheered. 'Goody gumdrops! Butch, steer the ship starboard and bring her about immediately. Keep your eyes peeled for an island. We're going treasure hunting!'

Butch didn't move – apart from his big burly knees, which were knocking together with fright. 'But, C-c-captain . . . what about the c-c-curse?' he said, his voice going wibbly-wobbly. 'C-c-cursed treasure sounds d-d-dangerous.'

'Codswallop,' scoffed the captain. 'If there's

treasure for the taking, then I'm the pirate to pilfer it. Hard starboard, I say – and see to it smartly. **Heave ho**!'

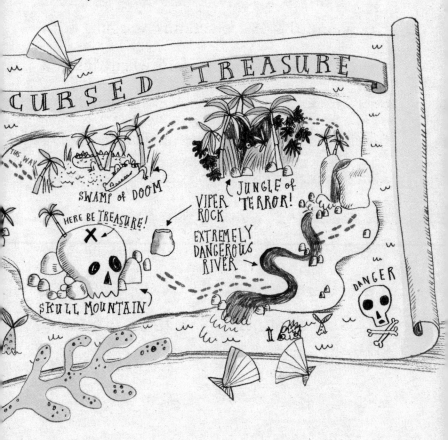

Chapter Two

Butch's shoulders slumped and he gave a little whimper, but he did as he was told. The captain *stamp*-clonked away while Ginger and Cannonball started picking up the potatoes.

Patch eyed Cutlass. 'Cursed treasure? Sounds a bit fishy . . .' she said worriedly. Then a dreamy smile rippled her whiskers. 'Mmmm . . . fish . . .' she sighed.

'**Arrrr**, wait, there's something left in the bottle!' Cutlass exclaimed, peering through the green glass. The bottle had rolled to a stop by the gunpowder barrels, and Patch padded over to see. Cutlass was right – it looked as if there was a *second* piece of paper inside.

Patch tried to push a paw into the bottle, but it didn't quite fit. Luckily, Ginger had left her fishing rod nearby – which had a sharp hook on the end – so Patch and Cutlass were able to catch and pull out the paper. As she unfolded it and saw what was scrawled there, Patch felt her fur tingle all over.

In red handwriting – was it *blood?* Patch wondered – was the following message:

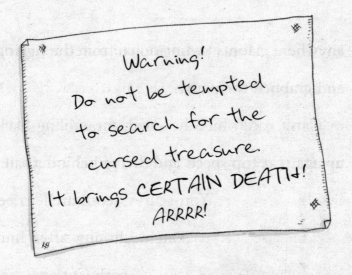

Warning!
Do not be tempted
to search for the
cursed treasure.
It brings CERTAIN DEATH!
ARRRR!

'What does it say, Cap'n? What does it say?' Cutlass asked, hopping from one foot to the other.

Patch read the warning aloud and they both shivered. 'Certain *death*?' Patch mewed, whiskers quivering. 'I don't fancy giving up any of my nine lives yet. We've got to show this to Halibut, at the double!'

But before they could take the warning

anywhere, Monty swung down from the rigging and grabbed the paper.

'Can't catch me!' he cried, scrambling back up again at top speed and diving behind a sail.

'You scurvy scoundrel!' cried Patch, chasing after him with Cutlass.

Giggling, Monty waved the paper in the air . . . but moments later the smirk was wiped right off his face when the wind snatched it from his paw and sent it spinning

out to sea.

'Whoops,' he gulped.

'No!' yowled Patch in dismay as

the paper bobbed on the

water for

a few moments, then sank

below the surface. 'Now the pirates won't get to

see the message – which means they won't know

about the warning of **CERTAIN DEATH**!'

'**ARRK**! What are we going to do?' squawked

Cutlass, flying around in circles.

Monty's lip quivered. 'I'm sorry, Cap'n

Patch,' he cried. 'I'm really ever so sorry!'

Captain Halibut, who was peering at the

treasure map nearby, looked up with a scowl.

Even though the animals could all understand each other perfectly well, when they spoke, it sounded to the pirates as if they were just meowing, squawking and making monkey noises.

'Stop that racket, for Davy Jones's sake,' he thundered, tossing his black curls with a dangerous glare. 'Or I'll introduce you to the nearest cannon!'

The captain's temper was enough to stop even the bravest of pirate cats, so Patch slunk off to the starboard side of the ship, with Cutlass flying beside her.

'This is a pirate pickle, all right,' Patch muttered, twitching her tail. 'We *can't* let the crew get their hands on the cursed treasure, Cutlass. We just can't!'

'You know what the captain's like about treasure, though,' Cutlass said worriedly.

Patch *did* know. Even in his sleep Captain Halibut would sometimes murmur about gold and silver and jewels.

'Well, somehow or other we're just going to have to make it extra difficult for the pirates to find the treasure,' she said. 'If we can only think up a super-sneaky plan first.'

'A super-sneaky plan,' Cutlass repeated. He cocked his head to one side and thought hard. 'Maybe if we map out a few ideas, we could—'

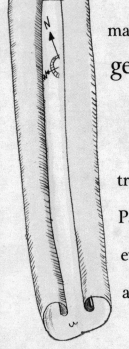

Patch clapped her paws together. 'The map – that's it!' she cried. 'You're a genius, Cutlass.'

'I am?' asked Cutlass in surprise.

'All we need to do is sneak that treasure map away from the pirates,' Patch explained, 'and then they won't even be able to find the *island*, let alone—'

'Land ahoy!' shouted Butch at that moment, his eye to the telescope. 'Treasure island straight ahead, Cap'n!' he bellowed. 'I found it!'

'Oh . . . ***poop decks***,' Patch cursed. 'And double poop decks!'

'Splendid,' replied Captain Halibut, striding over to join Butch. *Stamp-clonk, stamp-clonk*. Then he frowned, squinting into the distance. 'Shiver me timbers!' he shouted. 'Can it be true? Hand me that there telescope!'

Just then Ginger called, 'Ship ahoy!' from the crow's nest.

'Uh-oh,' said Butch, peering out to the horizon. 'Is that who I think it is?'

'It's the *Black Heart* and her terrible crew,' Captain Halibut replied grimly, a steely glint in his eye. 'And what, I would like to know, are *they* doing in these waters?'

Patch and Cutlass turned to look. Far in the distance they could just make out an island covered with palm trees and golden sands, with a skull-shaped mountain looming behind. And there, heading straight towards one of its coves, was a second pirate ship. Black sails fluttered from the ship's masts, with a ragged skull-and-crossbones flag flapping in the breeze right at the very top.

Butch's lower lip was wobbling. 'They must have heard about this treasure too, I reckon.' He shuffled nervously from foot to foot. 'And those *Black Heart* scoundrels are really scary. Really scary and *mean*!'

Cutlass edged closer to Patch. 'These pirates all look the same to me, Cap'n,' he confessed. 'Which ones are the *Black Heart* crew again?'

'They're led by the evil and villainous Captain Crunchbone,' Patch whispered in reply. 'Captain Halibut's biggest rival. There's no way Halibut will want *him* to get his hooks on the booty!'

Captain Halibut had indeed turned purple

at the sight of the enemy ship. 'Handsomely now, me hearties!' he roared, tattoos a-tremble. 'Full sail, I say! We've got to get to the treasure before Crunchbone – and that's an order!'

Patch felt her fur prickling. She had a bad feeling about this!

'Whatever Captain Halibut says, we *can't* let our crew get the cursed treasure,' she said to Cutlass. 'So we need to work out how to stop them – and fast!'

Chapter Three

Unfortunately for Patch, there was a wild westerly wind behind the *Golden Earring* that sent their ship speeding across the sea. But as swiftly as the *Golden Earring* sailed, it wasn't quite swift enough to catch up with the *Black Heart*.

'Hurry up, you bilge-sucking buffoons!' Captain Halibut howled to his crew as they saw the rival ship drop anchor ahead of them. 'They're getting away!' he groaned as the *Black Heart* pirates leaped triumphantly onto the island and charged off into the undergrowth.

'You never know, they might have just come here for a little holiday,' Ginger said. 'They might not even *like* treasure.'

'And anyway Cap'n, they don't have our map,' Cannonball reminded him.

'**Gaaah!** If I know Crunchbone, he'll have his own map,' Captain Halibut fumed, stamping up and down impatiently. 'But we must *not* let him steal my gold and silver and jewels.' He thumped a nearby cannon for good measure. *CLANG!* 'Do you hear me? That treasure is *mine* and I intend to claim it!'

'Aye aye, Cap'n,' said Butch, hunching over the ship's wheel and concentrating with all his twenty-seven brain cells as he steered the *Golden Earring* into port. 'The treasure's mine. Yep, got it.'

'*Mine*, not yours!' yelled the captain in exasperation. '*My* treasure! *MINE!*'

'That's what I said,' Butch replied, looking confused. 'My treasure. Mine. Anyway, here we are, Cap'n,' he added as the captain turned bright red and looked as if he was about to start shouting again. 'Lower the gangplank!'

'Anchor's away,' called Ginger, heaving it into the water with a SPLOSH.

Crouched near the bow, Patch and Cutlass peered out at the island while the pirates prepared to land. In front of them lay a wide golden beach, with dense forest and a rocky mountain further back. Brightly coloured parrots shrieked from the palm trees, and Cutlass waved a wing in greeting with a cheery 'Alright, lads?'

Patch took one look at the sandy beach and then stared down at her paws with a moggie shudder. She might be a pirate cat, but she hated getting sand in her fur. **UGH!**

Still – this was an important mission, she reminded herself. If they could stop the *Golden Earring* pirates claiming the cursed treasure, it would be well worth a spot of paw-licking later!

Down went the gang-plank and the crew hurried off the ship.

'The race is ON!' cried Captain Halibut as he charged towards the beach.

'Come on,' called Patch, scampering after the pirates, Cutlass flapping above her. 'You too, Monty. Stop picking your flea scabs and do something useful for once in your life.'

'Cheek,' sniffed Monty, but he bounded after them all the same.

Captain Halibut stopped on the beach to check the map, although not everyone was paying attention. Cutlass was hunting happily for sand worms, Butch was keeping a nervous eye on a scuttling hermit-crab and Ginger was rolling up her trouser legs and turning her face to the sun.

'Ahh,' she sighed, beaming. 'This is *lovely*. I'm going to get a smashing tan here, lads. Do you think there'll be anywhere we can get an ice lolly?'

'Cor!' cried Cannonball, picking up a pebble with a look of glee. 'I dunno about lollies, but check these out – rocks! Loads of 'em! I can make some rock cakes with these later – special treat!'

'You half-witted walrus, you don't use real rocks in rock cakes!' Captain Halibut snapped. 'You'll break all our teeth if you try. As for you, Ginger, get over here and help us with this map.

We're not hunting for lollies – we're hunting for treasure!'

Cutlass giggled to himself as he thought of a joke. 'I say, I say, I say,' he began to Patch. 'Why don't pirates get hungry when shipwrecked on a desert island?'

Why don't pirates get hungry when shipwrecked on a desert island?

Patch snorted. 'Everyone's hungry with a cook like Cannonball,' she replied.

'True,' agreed Cutlass. 'But on a desert island pirates *don't* get hungry . . . because of all the **sand which** *is there*. Sandwiches there! Get it, matey?'

Because of all the **sand which** is there.

He fluttered up in the air with a pleased-sounding squawk. 'Ha!'

'Good one,' laughed Patch, perching on a rock in order to stay off the hot sand. 'Okay, guys,' she said to Cutlass and Monty as the pirates crowded around the map, arguing and jabbing their fingers at it. 'We can't let our crew find the cursed treasure. So we need to stop them, or slow them down, any way we can.'

Monty pouted and began juggling shells. 'But I *want* some treasure,' he argued. 'A nice gold crown . . . King of the ship. Yeah, that would be cool!'

'Mmm, it *would* be cool, yes,' Patch agreed. Then she narrowed her eyes. 'Right until the curse kicks in and you're faced with

CERTAIN DEATH, that is! Monty, this is serious – we've got to stop them!'

Cutlass was pecking at a cuttle-fish bone on the sand, but flapped his wings excitedly as an idea came to him. 'Hey, I know – I'll peck a hole in the map!' he cried. 'I'll peck it to pieces!'

'YES, Cutlass!' cheered Patch. 'Great idea.

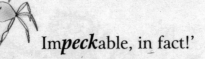

Im*peck*able, in fact!'

Without a map, the pirates wouldn't know *where* to search for the treasure. There was no way they'd be able to find it before the *Black Heart* crew!

Cutlass flew up into the air immediately and swooped towards the pirates, beak at the ready for some serious paper pecking. Down he hurtled . . . just as Captain Halibut leaned over to point at on the map, his big pirate hat blocking the flight path.

'Aarrrkk!' squawked Cutlass in alarm, swerving away at the last second and getting his feathers in a tangle.

'Get away, you poxy parrot!' cried Captain Halibut, swinging a fist through the air.

Monty laughed so hard he dropped his shells, but Patch was more encouraging.

'Try again,' she called.

Second time lucky, thought Patch as Cutlass flew up above the pirates once more, all set to tear into the map. Down he plunged . . . but this time *Butch* leaned over, getting his big bald bonce was in the way!

'Aarrrkk!' squawked Cutlass again, changing direction in the nick of time once more and feeling flustered as he landed on a nearby rock. Pecking holes in the map was proving to be harder than he'd imagined! Maybe he needed a better idea . . .

'Change of plan,' he announced. 'Watch this!'

Patch and Monty gazed on as, for a third time, their parrot pal flew across to where the pirates were standing in a huddle. This time, instead of pecking, Cutlass hovered right above the treasure map and then . . . **SPLAT!** A gooey parrot poo plopped all over the paper, covering every last detail.

'Eww!' cried Ginger, jumping back.

'It splashed me! It splashed me!' wailed Butch, diving into the sea to wash himself clean.

Patch was helpless with laughter. 'Genius!' she spluttered as Cutlass bowed in mid-air.

Cannonball peered at the parrot poo with interest. 'Is that . . . cream-cheese?' he asked, reaching a finger towards it.

'Pesky parrot!' yelled Captain Halibut, pushing Cannonball's hand away before his stupid cook could poison himself. 'Don't touch that, you blithering idiot. It's *not* cream-cheese!' He wiped the map on Cannonball's apron several times then squinted down at it. 'Oh, yuck, it's all smeary now,' he complained.

'Woo-hoo!' cheered Patch with a grin.

'But luckily I can still see *exactly* where we need to go,' said the captain, and Patch's whiskers wilted in disappointment. 'Now see here, me hearties, this is the way to the treasure. First we have to take fifty paces east until we reach the **Swamp of Doom**.'

Butch, who was returning from the sea, stopped dead as he heard this. 'Eek,' he said nervously.

'Then we make our way through the **Jungle of Terror**.'

'Yikes,' whimpered Butch.

'We cross the **Extremely Dangerous River**.'

'Wibble,' wibbled Butch.

'Walk twenty paces to **Viper Rock**.'

'Wahh,' wailed Butch.

'And then we climb **Skull Mountain**.'

'Noooooo,' squeaked Butch.

'Where **X** marks the spot! Well, that all sounds nice and easy for an old salt like me,' said the captain, putting the map in his pocket.

Patch pulled a face at Cutlass. 'Nice and easy? It sounds absolutely horrible!' she hissed, glancing longingly back at the *Golden Earring*, where there were no swamps, no jungles and where the deadliest danger came from Cannonball's dinners.

'If they even get to the treasure in one piece it'll be a miracle,' Cutlass added, with a shake of his head.

'**Swamp of Doom** coming right up,

buckos!' the captain cried, clapping his hands together. 'So – fifty paces east. Who knows how to count?'

'Um . . .' said Ginger doubtfully. 'I can do up to three. I think!'

'I can count up to eleventy hundred,' Butch boasted. 'Let's go!'

Chapter Four

The pirates set off across the beach, with Patch, Cutlass and Monty racing after them, over the sand and on to a path that led into the trees. The undergrowth was thick and steamy, with strange colourful flowers blooming in the bushes and hairy coconuts dangling from palm trees above.

Patch almost collided with Butch's legs as he came to a sudden standstill.

'Nobody panic,' Butch said, voice shaking, 'but . . . **HEEEELP!** There's a great huge scary s-s-s-spider! Nobody told me there would be s-s-s-spiders in here!' His knees knocked together as he pointed at an enormous cobweb that stretched its sticky strands across the path, with a gigantic black furry spider perched in one corner.

Patch pulled a face. She was quite fond of *catching* spiders, but did *not* like getting cobwebs in her whiskers. Yuck!

'Allow me!' said Cannonball, searching in his apron pocket. 'Aha!' he cried, pulling out a bread knife in triumph and setting about the web. *SLASH!* went the knife through the sticky strands. *SLASH! SLASH!*

Soon the cobweb dangled from the bushes in tatters. The spider was extremely cross about this and promptly scuttled up the leg of Butch's shorts, causing him to scream and dance about in terror. 'Ooh! Ahh! It's got me!' he screeched, right until Cannonball whopped him over the head with his ladle. *CLANG!*

'Let's get ahead of them,' hissed Patch to her gang as the pirates started arguing. 'We might be able to find something else to slow down the crew.'

Off they hurried . . . and of course Monty, the show-off, couldn't help trying to go faster than the others. He charged ahead, swinging through the trees, until he stopped suddenly in front of a wooden sign stuck in the ground.

He turned in alarm, calling to the other two,
'We've got to hurry! There's *sand*!'

'Sand?' Patch repeated, wrinkling her nose
as she approached. More sand? Had they
somehow looped round to another beach? Oh,
she hoped not!

'Look – on the sign,' Monty said importantly.
'Quick! Sand!'

Patch burst out laughing. 'It doesn't mean *we* have to be quick, you silly banana,' she chuckled. 'It's *quicksand* – you'll sink if you try to walk across it. Arrrr, this must be the **Swamp of Doom**.'

Monty put his nose in the air and turned away. 'Am NOT a silly banana,' he huffed.

The swamp was boggy and marshy, with a salty, rotting smell. Mosquitoes buzzed lazily above the surface. Cutlass shivered and pointed a wing-tip to where a pirate hat was just visible in the middle of the quicksand. 'Looks like someone was unlucky there,' he said. 'I wonder if the *Black Heart* crew came this way?'

Patch stepped back at once. 'We don't want that to happen to our pirates,' she said, thinking hard, 'but maybe if they got stuck just for a *little* while it would slow them up enough to miss out on the cursed treasure!'

'Clever!' cried Cutlass, fluttering a loop-the-loop. 'Then we can rescue them and they'll be so happy and grateful they might even get me some bird seed.'

'And me some fish,' Patch agreed, her eyes going all dreamy at the thought. '**Mmmm** . . . **fish** . . .'

'Eleventy-five . . . eleventy-nine . . . er . . . twelvety-six,' came the voice of Butch in the distance. The pirates were catching up with them!

'Hurry! Let's block the sign so they walk right into the quicksand!' Patch cried, leaping up on top of it and draping her paws over the letters.

"Eleventy - five... eleventy - nine... er... TWELVETY-SIX..."

Cutlass hovered in mid-air in front of the sign, his wings stretched out wide.

But Monty was still in a big fat sulk about being called a silly banana and didn't feel like helping one bit. In fact, as the pirates rounded the corner, he sneaked up and gave Patch an almighty **PUSH** instead, so that she lost her balance and toppled off the sign . . . right into the sloppy quicksand!

SQUELCH!

'Help!' yowled Patch.

Cutlass flapped around, trying to tow her out by tugging at her eye patch, but it slipped from his beak and twanged back against Patch's head.

'OW!'

'Sorry!'

'*FIFTY!*' cried Butch in relief, reaching the sign.

'Monty, you stinking scallywag,' Patch spluttered, thrashing about hopelessly. Try as she might to escape, she could feel her paws slipping deeper and deeper into the quicksand. She scrabbled and scrambled, but soon she was up to her tummy in the swamp. Any minute

now her head would sink beneath the surface
and then . . .

'Here – grab this,' cried Cutlass, who'd
managed to drop a branch down to her.

Patch clung on shakily and, claw by claw, she
hauled herself out until she was safely back on
firm ground.

'That monkey. Just wait till I get my paws on him,' she growled, trying to shake the smelly wet sand out of her fur. 'He's going to be **SOOO** sorry!'

Of course, Monty was laughing so hard that he was rolling around on the ground and not looking sorry at *all.*

The other pirates had caught up with Butch by now. 'A sign!' cried Ginger, pointing at it with excitement.

'Does it say *TREASURE*?' asked the captain, peering to read the letters.

'Nope,' said Cannonball. 'It says—'

'Ooh, does it say *CUSTARD*?' interrupted Ginger hopefully, jigging up and down.

Cutlass rolled his eyes. 'I say, I say, I say:

why don't pirates know their alphabet, Cap'n?'

Why don't pirates know their alphabet, Cap'n?

he asked Patch in a low voice. 'Because they always get stuck at C. Get it, matey? Stuck at **SEA**!'

'The sign says *QUICKSAND*!' replied Cannonball, and he held out a rolling pin to block the way. 'This must be the **Swamp of Doom**. Nobody take another step forward!'

'**Nobody take another step forward!**' repeated Captain Halibut, who hated anyone else giving orders.

Because they always get stuck at C. Stuck at SEA!

55

'Not even a single toe!'

Butch leaped backwards at once, teeth chattering nervously. 'This place gives me the heebie-jeebies,' he whimpered.

Ginger flicked a creepy-crawly off her ear. 'Where next, Captain?' she asked. 'I hope it's going to be nicer than the **Swamp of Doom**.'

Captain Halibut took out the map and checked the route. 'Arrrr, next we need to head through the **Jungle of Terror**,' he replied. 'Sounds a doddle to me. Mark my words, we'll have this treasure in the blink of a squid's eye!'

'Unless the *Black Heart* pirates have got there first, that is,' Cannonball pointed out, rather unhelpfully. 'Look – footprints! Do you think that was them?'

'Gah!' growled Captain Halibut, gnashing his teeth together at the sight of the footprints leading away into the jungle. Then he began *stamp*-clonking furiously after them. 'What are you shower of shellfish waiting for?' he yelled over his shoulder. '**Move it**!'

The pirates set off again, followed by Monty, who turned round to titter at Patch and Cutlass. 'Patch, that is one special fur-do you've got going on,' he smirked. 'It really suits you!'

Patch glared after him. She was still damp and sticky from the quicksand and could feel her fur standing up in spikes.

'Oh, ha ha,' she hissed crossly, before turning back to her feathered friend. 'We'll have to keep trying, Cutlass,' she said. 'Anything to stop the pirates getting their mitts on the cursed treasure. Come on, there has to be another way to slow them down!'

As the crew ventured into the **Jungle of Terror**, the pirates quickly realized that it *was* a pretty terrible place.

TWANGGG! BOINGGG!

Patch and Cutlass sent jungle vines

snapping into

the pirates'

faces.

BOOF!

THUD!

Patch and Cutlass

dropped coconuts onto the pirates' heads.

SLITHER! SLAP! Patch and Cutlass

pushed tree snakes off the branches so that

they fell squiggling and

squirming onto

the pirates'

shoulders.

'Wah! I don't like it here,' Butch yelped as a large green snake hissed in his ear.

'It's as if the **Jungle of Terror** wants to, you know, *terrify* us,' agreed Ginger, rubbing her head where a coconut had bounced off it.

'Yeah, like someone's trying to tell us something,' Cannonball shuddered, using a spatula to fight through the springy vines.

'Nobody panic, but the map *did* say that the treasure was **cursed**,' Butch reminded them in a small, scared voice.

'Do you think . . . do you think all these bad things are happening because of the *curse*?' asked Cannonball fearfully.

Patch and Cutlass grinned at each other and

60

did one of their secret high-fives, paw to claw. Their plan was working! Any minute now the pirates would admit defeat and return to the ship, and they'd all be safe from the **cursed treasure**!

But just then . . .

'Codswallop! Balderdash! Nonsense!' snorted Captain Halibut. 'Someone's trying to tell you something? Yes, it's me, trying to tell you lot to stop being such a pack of **ninnies**. Now pull yourselves together and keep walking. The sun's shining! We're having an adventure, like proper pirates and we're going to get that treasure if it's the last thing we do!'

Chapter Five

On went the pirates, hacking through the jungle. Birds made mournful calls to one another from the trees. Lizards scuttled away at the sound of the pirates' **heavy** footsteps. Every now and then a huge, horrible skull could be seen at the side of the path. It didn't exactly feel a friendly place to be.

After a few minutes, Patch spotted a red-bottomed baboon high up in a tree nearby and had another idea. 'Arrrr,' she hissed to Cutlass. 'New plan. Let's see if *this* slows the pirates down.' She raced ahead and scrambled up the nearest palm tree. Still wet and bedraggled, she made her one green eye look wide and frightened, yowling her most pathetic meows. 'Meow! Meow! MEOWWWW!'

The pirates stopped dead.

'I thought I just heard a cow,' said Butch, scratching his head and looking around nervously. 'And don't panic anyone, but cows are really massive and scary.'

'It wasn't a cow – it was a cat,' argued Cannonball, gazing around too. Then he licked his lips. 'If it's a big cat, we could be in for a special treat for dinner tonight,' he went on. 'A few tiger chunks would go *very* nicely in my tentacle stew, I can tell you. Even better, a delicious juicy lion chop!'

'Meoowwwww,' wailed Patch miserably from above their heads. **'Meooowww!'**

'It's not a lion or a tiger – it's *our* cat. It's Patch!' cried Ginger, pointing upwards. 'Awww, look! She's stuck, poor thing.'

They all stared up at Patch in the tree.

'Oh well, never mind. That's one less mouth to feed,' said Captain Halibut heartlessly. 'Back to the treasure hunt!'

'We can't just leave her here in the middle of nowhere!' protested Butch. 'With all those snakes and spiders and cows and that!'

Captain Halibut rolled his eyes. 'All right, one of you climb up and rescue the silly creature then,' he said. 'But hurry up about it.'

'Me!' said Ginger, sticking her hand up at once. 'Me! Pick me! I love climbing. I'll do it!'

'Butch, you can do it,' said the captain, ignoring Ginger. 'And get a move on. If the *Black Heart* pirates have somehow managed to get their hands on my treasure, there'll be trouble.' He drew a finger across his throat with a fierce scowl.

'**MEOOOOWWWWW**,' wailed Patch, huddling against the trunk of the tree.

'Aye aye, Cap'n,' said Butch, striding over. 'All right, there kitty, don't you fret. Big brave Butch will have you down in no time.' He began hauling himself up the tree, his huge knees gripping the trunk.

Patch edged away, onto a long branch that stretched out over a clump of thorny bushes.

'Here, kitty kitty,' Butch crooned, clambering after her. But Butch was big and heavy . . . and the branch was thin and twiggy . . . As Butch teetered along it, there was a *CREAK*. And then a *CRACK*.

Patch leaped higher into the tree just as the branch went sn*ap* . . . and Butch went tumbling down into the thorny bushes below.

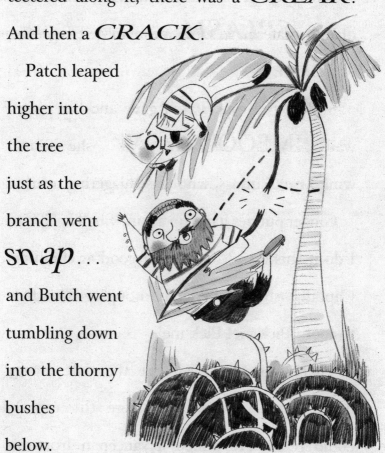

'YOW! OW! EE! MUMMY!' he yelled, springing out again, falling over and rolling into the undergrowth. The other pirates heard what sounded like a small avalanche followed by a distant *SPLASH* and then everything went quiet.

Still in the tree, Patch gave another pitiful wail. 'MEOOOOWW!' she cried, winking at Cutlass, who was sniggering nearby.

Ginger put her hand up again. 'Shall I go? Can I do it this time? I'm proper good at climbing, Captain!' she cried eagerly, hopping from foot to foot. 'Pick me! Pick me!'

'Arrrr, watch. This'll get the daft moggy down,' said Cannonball before the captain could reply. He pulled a saucepan from his apron pocket, closed one eye and took aim . . .

. . . just as Cutlass, sensing his pal was about to get panned, flew quickly over and pecked Cannonball on the end of his nose.

'**YOWCH!**' yelped Cannonball, losing his balance and sending the saucepan spinning off in the wrong direction. 'My best pan!' he cried in dismay as it disappeared into the bushes.

Sensing the chance to get in Cannonball's good books – and earn himself some extra bananas – Monty went bounding helpfully after the pan, while Ginger turned her attention to the captain once more. '*Now* shall I try? Is it my turn? Oh, *please* let me try!'

'Oh, go on then. If you must,' the captain grumbled. 'But hurry up, otherwise we'll have to leave that **stupid** moggy behind. And good riddance.'

Charming, thought Patch, flicking her tail crossly as Ginger began scrambling up the tree.

Unlike Butch, Ginger was light, nimble and used to climbing up to the crow's nest back on the ship. Up she went, fast and fearless, all the way until she was very nearly at the top.

'Actually, I think I'll just jump down myself,' Patch mewed, leaping lightly past Ginger to the ground.

'Oh!' cried Ginger in surprise, then she beamed. 'Yay, I did it!' she called, clambering back down again. 'I rescued the cat!'

'Who's a clever little thing?' said Cannonball just at that moment.

Ginger jumped happily to the ground – she had never been called clever before! But then her face fell as she realized that Cannonball was talking to *Monty*, who'd sprung out from the bushes clutching the cook's rather battered saucepan.

'What a smart lad you are. You've always been my favourite,' Cannonball went on,

ruffling Monty's fur. Patch and Cutlass pulled faces at each other as Monty preened himself proudly. He was a sickening suck-up – he really was!

Seconds later, Butch appeared, dripping wet but beaming all over his face. 'Hey, good news – I found the river!' he cried.

'The **Extremely Dangerous River**? *Marvellous* news!' cheered Captain Halibut. 'Lead on, Butch. Not too much further to go, buckos. I can almost smell that treasure now!'

If there was one thing Patch hated even more than having sandy paws, it was having wet paws. So when they reached the **Extremely Dangerous River** and she realized that there wasn't a nice dry bridge across it her heart sank down to her claws. The river was a murky brown colour, so you couldn't see what lay at the bottom, and it smelled of dead things. As the pirates rolled up their trouser legs and began wading through, Patch had to act fast to avoid being left behind. There was really only one thing for it: she was going to have to hitch a ride. Ginger wouldn't mind a furry passenger, would she?

'Erk!' cried Ginger the next second, as Patch leaped on to her shoulders. 'Ow, those claws are *sharp*!'

'Come on pirates, keep walking while you're talking,' the captain ordered, striding through the stinking water. 'And watch out for crocodiles.'

73

Butch came next, then Cannonball, then Ginger. *Splosh. Splash. Splosh.* Cutlass flew overhead, but Monty was left behind on the shore.

'Hey! Wait for me!' he cried, jumping up and down.

Patch giggled from her perch on Ginger. 'Can't you swim?' she teased.

'Of course I can't. I'm a monkey not a monkfish!' wailed Monty.

'If only you hadn't pushed me in that quicksand, I *might* have helped you,' Patch said, 'but instead . . . **byeee!**' She waved a paw cheekily at him, then clambered up onto Ginger's head, turning round a few times in order to get comfortable.

'Patch, sit still – I can't see when you do that!'
Ginger complained, trying to push Patch's tail
out of her face as she waded along. 'In fact, I . . .
Whoops!'

Whoops indeed! Ginger had stumbled blindly
forward and knocked straight into Cannonball.

Cannonball bumped into Butch.

Butch lurched into the captain and . . .
SPLOSH!

Down the captain tumbled onto his hands
and knees, instantly soaked through by the
pongy brown water.

Just to make matter worse, Monty, seeing
his chance to get across the **Extremely
Dangerous River**, used the pirates as
stepping stones, jumping from one to the other.

Boing! Boing! Boing! LEAP!

'I can't swim, but at least I've got a brain,' he chuckled to Patch as he reached the other side, doing a handstand on the grass and waggling his bottom.

Still in the river, the pirates had gone very quiet at the sight of their soggy captain.

'Uh-oh,' mumbled Butch.

'Now we're in for it,' whimpered Cannonball.

'He's going to be really, *really* mad!' groaned Ginger.

'I don't believe it,' said the captain, not moving as he kneeled there in the water. 'I do NOT believe it.'

'I'm really extremely and truly sorry, Captain,' Ginger said in a squeaky voice.

'It was an accident,' Cannonball added meekly.

'It wasn't me – it was the others. They pushed me,' Butch quavered.

'Well, it wasn't *me*! It was Ginger!' protested Cannonball, glaring back at her.

'It wasn't me either! It was the cat!' cried Ginger, and Patch hunched lower on Ginger's head, fearing that she was in for a mighty telling-off.

'The cat, eh?' repeated Captain Halibut, and Patch tried to make herself even smaller. The captain had a fearsome temper when he was angry and anything could happen. He might make her walk the plank. He might leave her here on this desert island. He might even feed her to the nearest shark!

'Well, blow me down, that mangy moggy just did us all one blisteringly big favour,' boomed Captain Halibut, much to Patch's surprise. He rose to a standing position, shook the water from his beard and clambered out of the river.

'Because if I hadn't been pushed over like that I wouldn't have put my hand on THIS!'

He held up a small gold key that sparkled in the sunlight and the other pirates edged nearer curiously.

'I thought for a moment it was a fish,' the captain went on, gazing at it fondly. 'But no, it's not a fish.'

Patch glanced at Cutlass uncertainly. 'Is it me or is he being a bit . . . odd?' she hissed.

'Arrrr, reckon he must have bumped his head when he fell down,' Cutlass agreed.

The other pirates all seemed confused about Halibut's behaviour as well.

'No,' Butch replied cautiously. 'It's not a fish, Cap'n.'

'Can't have *that* with chips,' Cannonball confirmed. 'Well, you could, I suppose, but I'm not sure it would taste all that good. Maybe with a bit of ketchup or vinegar, it might—'

'It's a key,' Ginger interrupted before Cannonball could say anything else, 'with a weird skull shape at the top.'

'Exactly!' Captain Halibut cried. 'Just like the skull drawing on our map! Aharr! So, unless I'm very much mistaken, this is the key to a treasure chest. *My* treasure chest.' He gave the key a smacking kiss then punched the air. 'Even if the *Black Heart* pirates *do* get to the treasure first, those rotten old crooks won't be able to open the chest without this. What a stroke of luck!' The captain was practically skipping around with glee. 'So hurry up and haul yourselves out of this here river, you lumbering layabouts – and let's track down our booty!'

Chapter Six

With a lot of **splashing** and **sploshing** and some very wet trousers, the pirates clambered out of the **Extremely Dangerous River** and not a moment too soon, as a crocodile appeared from further up the bank, its long snout poking hungrily from the water. Butch screamed and tried to jump into Ginger's arms.

Cannonball grabbed a cheese grater and tried to shoo the crocodile away.

And Captain Halibut, who was starting to lose his patience, shouted, 'For Davy Jones's sake!

It's a floating log, not a crocodile, you jittering jellyfish. Look!' He kneeled down on the bank of the river and stretched out an arm to prod the 'log' with a stick . . . except, of course, it *wasn't* a log – it definitely *was* a crocodile, with big, sharp teeth and a very hungry belly. **SNAP!** went the crocodile's jaws, just missing the captain, who promptly fell backwards in alarm.

Patch and Cutlass laughed their heads off at this, and Patch even found herself cheering up a little bit about the key.

'I say, I say, I say: what kind of key *doesn't* unlock a treasure chest?'

What kind of key doesn't unlock a treasure chest?

Cutlass squawked to Patch as Halibut coughed and dusted himself down and the other pirates tried not to snigger.

'Hopefully the one that Captain Halibut just found,' Patch replied, twitching her whiskers.

'The answer is . . . a **mon**key!' said Cutlass, pointing a wing towards Monty, who was dangling upside down from a nearby tree. 'A *mon-key* – get it, matey?' He grinned as Patch groaned

A monkey!

and rolled her eyes. 'You have to get up early to key-p up with my jokes, Cap'n,' he added.

'So where are we heading next?' asked Ginger as the crew set off once more. 'I hope it's somewhere really, really nice this time. Is it?'

'We're heading west,' Captain Halibut replied, checking the map. 'All the way to **Viper Rock**. After that, we hike up **Skull Mountain** and then . . . **X** marks the spot!'

Butch stopped walking. 'Viper Rock?' he repeated. 'More snakes? Aww, man! Can't I just stay here and wait for you guys to come back with the treasure?'

'There's no need to be scared,' Cannonball scoffed. 'I could wrestle a viper with my bare hands. I could tie one in a *knot*. If a viper dared try anything with me, I'd simply look it in the eye and say, "Don't you even think about it, sunshine." You've just got to be tough, that's all. Show 'em who's boss.'

'I say, I say, I say,' Cutlass chuckled to Patch. 'How does a snake keep its car clean? With **vindscreen vipers**! Get it, matey? With w—WHOA!' He shot up high in the air suddenly, his feathers a-flap. 'Vipers at three o'clock!' he yelped.

How does a snake keep its car clean?

With vindscreen vipers!

87

Turning to see what had startled him, Patch almost jumped out of her fur as she saw three enormous snakes sliding down from a huge red rock nearby, their forked tongues flicking in and out. Her tail tingled with terror and she galloped away at once, pelting along the path to safety with Cutlass flapping overhead.

'Run, Monty!' she yelled.

Behind them, she heard a screech from Butch. 'Nobody panic,' he squealed. 'But –

HELP! Poisonous, murdering snakes with fangs and poison and really mean little beady eyes! Everyone hide behind Cannonball!' He ducked behind the tough, snake-wrestling cook at once, knees knocking. So did Ginger. Even Captain Halibut scurried fearfully behind

his crew with a very quick
stamp-clonk, *stamp-clonk*.

Cannonball looked at
the vipers. The vipers
looked at Cannonball.

'Go on, what are you
waiting for, you scurvy
dog?' yelled Captain
Halibut. 'Tie those snakes
in knots at **ONCE**! Plait
them if you want – I don't
care!'

The vipers were coming
closer, hissing alarmingly.
But Cannonball did not
wrestle them with his bare

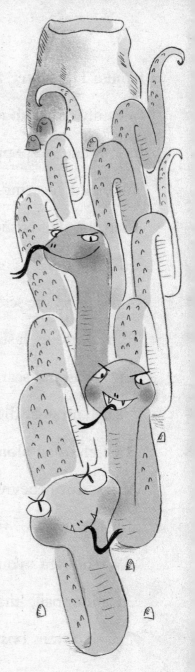

hands. He didn't tie them in knots. And he certainly didn't show them who was boss. No. In fact, sweat had popped up all over Cannonball's shiny pink face and he was quivering like a jelly. Then the snakes slid even nearer and he let out a shrill shriek.

'RUN!' he screamed at the top of his voice. 'Run, now, as fast as you can! They're really dangerous and scary! **Aaarrrgghhhhh!**'

The pirates did not need telling twice. They charged along the path, away from the vipers, until they were red in the face and out of breath.

'I thought you said,' Butch panted to Cannonball, 'that you just had to show 'em who was boss? That you could wrestle 'em, and talk to 'em, and tie 'em up in knots, and . . .'

'He got muddled up with his shoelaces,' Patch giggled to Cutlass and Monty as they rounded the corner and found themselves at the foot of a mountain.

'Those were the wrong sort of vipers,' Cannonball told Butch in a huffy sort of way. 'Any other viper – yeah. No problem. I'd have dealt with them.' He coughed and looked down at his feet. 'Anyway,' he went on, before anyone could argue with him. 'Look! A mountain!'

'Excellent,' cried Captain Halibut, checking the map. 'This must be **Skull Mountain**. We're nearly there, team! Now all we need to do is climb up, look for an **X** and dig up the buried treasure!'

'Cool!' said Ginger, skipping nimbly up the rocks. Then she stopped as a thought occurred to her. 'Um . . . wait. Digging? Did anyone bring a spade?'

'Well, I didn't,' said Butch.

'And I didn't,' Captain Halibut said. 'Cannonball?'

'I've got . . .

a fish-slice . . .

a meat

cleaver . . .

a wooden

spoon . . .'

Cannonball

replied, searching

92

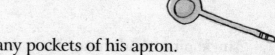

through the many pockets of his apron.

'How about a spade?'

'A spatula . . . a lemon squeezer . . . a frying pan . . .'

'A *spade*?'

'A potato peeler . . . an apple corer . . . a really good little non-stick milk pan if anyone fancies cocoa . . .'

'But no spade?' the captain asked impatiently.

Cannonball shook his head. 'Sorry, Cap'n. No spade.'

Patch, Cutlass and Monty edged away as they saw the captain's moustache stand on end with fury. And yet Patch could feel a giggle in her throat too. They'd come all this way – they had almost reached the treasure! – and yet not one

93

single pirate had thought to bring along a spade to actually dig it up. It seemed more likely than ever that the cursed treasure was not about to come their way, so everyone would be safe from the **CERTAIN DEATH** that the paper in the bottle had warned them about!

'Why oh why,' the captain was complaining, 'am I stuck with such a bunch of utter **nincompoops** and **nitwits** for my crew? Of all the **brainless**, blundering **buffoons**, you lot really take the biscuit! I can't believe—' He fell silent. 'What was that?'

They all stopped to listen as the sound of cheerful singing floated down the mountain towards them.

'Yo-ho-ho, and a bottle of rum,

We've got the treasure, yum yum yum!

The Black Heart *crew are the richest at sea,*

Yo-ho-ho, happy pirates are we!'

Patch and Cutlass looked at each other. 'Does that mean . . . ?' Cutlass began hopefully.

'I think we did it!' Patch beamed. 'We slowed down our crew so much that the *Black Heart* pirates beat them to the cursed treasure!'

'What, so I'm not going to get my crown?' Monty sighed. 'Huh! That's not fair!'

Butch, meanwhile, was humming the tune under his breath. He was very fond of a pirate shanty, even though he nearly always got the words wrong.

'That's a jolly song,' he commented. 'And they're the richest pirates – well, that's nice, ain't it?'

Captain Halibut wheeled round in rage. 'That's *nice*? You **dunderbrain**, did you not listen to the words they were singing? They've got the treasure! *Our* treasure! They made it there before us – and *they* clearly remembered to take spades with them!' He stamped his peg leg so hard that Patch thought for a moment it was going to crack in two. 'And now they're heading back to their ship with our loot!' he roared. He pointed into the distance where they could just see glimpses of pirate hats bobbing above the bushes. 'There they are. After them, me hearties!'

The captain charged off in the direction of the singers, with Butch, Cannonball and Ginger rushing along behind. Then Halibut stopped suddenly, a finger to his lips, and they all cannoned into the back of him.

'Shhh,' he whispered. 'We've got to be quiet about this. Don't let them know we're following them. Got it?'

'Got it, Captain,' said Ginger.

'Aye aye,' agreed Cannonball.

'Quietly does it,' said Butch, going up on to tiptoes and promptly falling over into a prickly bush with a crash and a loud 'OW!'.

Patch sighed. 'I suppose we should go along too,' she said. 'Try to stop them getting into any more trouble.'

'See if I can just sneak a teeny tiny gold crown or something as well . . .' Monty added hopefully under his breath.

Captain Halibut, Butch, Cannonball and Ginger began creeping silently through the jungle after the *Black Heart* pirates, hiding behind trees and bushes as they went, with Patch, Cutlass and Monty at their heels. The *Black Heart* pirates were noisy and cheerful and didn't have a clue they were being followed as they hauled along the treasure chest, singing at the tops of their voices and swigging from a bottle of grog.

Their smallest pirate had tufty black hair and seemed to be struggling with the heavy chest.

'Lads, can we stop for a break?' he puffed, red in the face. He staggered on the uneven ground and the chest lurched against the other pirates.

'Good idea,' hiccupped the tallest crew member, who had a feathered earring and seemed to have drunk quite a lot of the grog.

'This here looks a bonny spot,' declared Captain Crunchbone as they arrived at a clearing just then. He was tall and fierce-looking with a bushy red beard, a gold front tooth and a bone through his nostrils. 'Arrrr, take the weight off for a few minutes, me hearties.'

The *Black Heart* pirates dumped the chest on the ground and flopped down around it, panting and sweating. The smallest pirate put his thumb in his mouth and fell asleep at once. The tallest pirate put his hat over his face and began to snore. Captain Crunchbone leaned against the treasure chest, stretched out his long legs and shut his eyes, while the rest of his crew dozed in the jungle sunshine.

Hiding in the undergrowth, Captain Halibut beamed so widely that his gold tooth sparkled in the sun. 'This is our chance,' he hissed to the crew, then held up the key. 'We creep over, quiet as ship's mice. We open the chest, quiet as ship's mice. We steal all the treasure, quiet as ship's mice. We make a run for it all the way back to the *Golden Earring*, fast as gunfire. Then we sail away, rich as princes!'

'Yay!' cried Ginger excitedly, before remembering that they were meant to be quiet and slapping a hand across her mouth.

Luckily, Captain Halibut was too busy sniggering at his own good fortune to notice. 'They even dug the chest up for us,' he chortled. 'Who needs spades anyway?'

A small distance away, Patch addressed Cutlass and Monty. 'This is *our* chance too,' she said. 'As soon as our pirates start creeping over, we make as much noise as we can. Yowling, screeching, squawking . . . whatever it takes to wake up the *Black Heart* crew. Got it?'

'Aye aye, Cap'n!' chirped Cutlass, flapping his wings. 'I can fly in and peck them all awake.'

'I can sneak in and steal a crown,' Monty said stubbornly.

'No!' cried Patch and Cutlass at the same time. 'Please, Monty,' Patch added, as the *Golden Earring* pirates began tiptoeing towards the treasure. 'Trust me on this! Leave the treasure well alone and I'll . . . I'll smuggle some bananas out of the kitchen for you when we're back on board ship.'

Monty wrinkled his nose. 'Hmm,' he said. 'But I wanted a crown.'

(Meanwhile, slowly and silently, the *Golden Earring* pirates had reached the chest.)

'Then I'll . . . I'll *make* you a crown,' Cutlass said desperately. 'A really cool pirate crown, out of feathers . . . and shells . . . and . . .'

'And fish bones!' Patch added helpfully. 'How about that?' Then her eyes went all glassy for a moment. '**Mmmm . . . fish . . .**' she sighed.

Monty scratched his flea scabs, considering. 'Hmm,' he said again.

(Meanwhile, slowly and silently, Captain Halibut was sliding the

small golden key into the treasure-chest lock. *Click!* It fitted perfectly.)

'Well?' Patch hissed. 'What do you think? You'll help us and you won't try to take any of the cursed treasure – and in return, we'll do those things for you?'

'And I'll be king of the ship?' Monty persisted.

Patch growled in her throat. 'You'll be king of the ship,' she promised, just as Captain Halibut lifted the lid of the treasure chest. Patch blinked at the dazzling heap of gold and silver and jewels inside – goblets, trinkets and crowns, all glittering and gleaming in the light.

'Hello, my beauties,' whispered Captain Halibut in wonder. 'You're mine now. All mine!'

'Do we have a deal?' Patch asked Monty urgently.

'Okaaaaay,' grumbled Monty.

'Thank goodness for that,' said Patch. 'Now, let's make some noise!'

Chapter Seven

'MEOWWWWW! YOWWWLLLLL!'

went Patch, leaping out into the clearing, her fur on end.

'SQUAWK! SCREECH! SHRIEK!'

went Cutlass, swooping down to peck the *Black Heart* pirates awake.

'OOOH! OOH! AHH! AHH! GIBBER GIBBER OOH AHH!' went Monty, capering about excitedly, throwing pebbles and sticks around.

'What the . . . ? Whoa!'

'Wait!'

'**What?**' yelled the *Black Heart* pirates as they woke up, one by one.

'**Thieves!**'

'**Villains!**'

'**Grab the treasure and run!**'

Captain Crunchbone leaped to his feet with a mighty roar of rage. 'Oh no you don't!' he bellowed. He slammed the lid of the treasure chest shut with a bone-shaking *BANG* then pushed Captain Halibut flat on his back.

'Wargh!' cried Halibut, whacking his head on the grog bottle.

The *Black Heart* pirates grabbed the chest and charged off back towards the beach at top speed. The *Golden Earring* pirates raced after them, thundering through the jungle with bloodthirsty war cries. Patch, Cutlass and Monty had no choice but to rush along too, with Patch desperately hoping that the rival pirates would beat her own crew.

THUMP! BUMP! THUD! Captain Halibut's team took a wrong turn and tumbled into a deep pit.

'Ha ha!' jeered the *Black Heart* pirates, racing to cross a rocky river and leaving them behind.

But as soon as the *Golden Earring* crew had scrambled out of the pit, they discovered a nifty shortcut by swinging on vines across the river.

'Wheeeeeee! Whooaaaaaa!' cried Patch, clinging on with every claw.

'Ha HA!' yelled Captain Halibut as they closed in on the enemy again.

By the time they were back on the sandy beach, the rival crews were neck and neck. 'Arrrr! You horrible hammerhead! Hand over my treasure or ELSE!' bellowed Captain Halibut, in such a terrifying voice that Patch's pointy ears trembled and Butch had a little accident.

'You'll have to fight us for it!' yelled back Captain Crunchbone, shooting a blunderbuss into the air with a mighty **BOOM! CRACK!** Then came the swishing of silver blades as every single member of his crew pulled out shiny cutlasses and swung them aloft.

'They mean business, all right,' said Patch to Cutlass in alarm, as the *Black Heart* pirates took three steps forward, with menacing expressions on their faces.

'Weapons, crew, weapons!' cried Captain Halibut, patting his pockets as he and the *Golden Earring* pirates took three steps back. 'Who's got our weapons?'

'Um . . .' said Cannonball, holding out a rolling pin.

'I've got *this* . . .'

'And I've got . . . er . . . *these*,' offered Ginger, clenching her puny little fists.

'And I've got . . . a really, really bad feeling in my tummy and I'm going to run away now. Byeeee!' cried Butch, turning and sprinting for the safety of the ship. **'Waahhhhhh!'**

'Er . . .' said Captain Halibut desperately. 'We . . . er . . . could toss a coin for the treasure? Arm-wrestle, maybe?'

The *Black Heart* pirates burst out laughing.

'Ha ha ha ha ha ha! Toss a coin, he says. I don't *think* so, matey,' snarled Captain Crunchbone. 'Go on, you pack of chumps, before I *really* give you something to squeal about. Sling your hooks. We won the treasure, fair and square.

And we're gonna keep it.' He sniggered. 'By the way, thanks for finding the key for us. Very helpful of you.'

Captain Halibut's shoulders slumped in defeat. So did Ginger's. Cannonball tucked his rolling pin back in his apron pocket with a sigh. Then the three of them turned and trudged towards the *Golden Earring* with heavy hearts, all thinking glumly about the gold and silver and jewels that had so nearly been theirs.

Patch, Cutlass and Monty followed, glancing back to see the *Black Heart* pirates loading the treasure chest onto their ship with cheers and another round of singing.

'YES, crew,' said Patch in relief. 'We

did it. Between us, we actually did it. **ARRRR**!'

'We totally saved the day,' Cutlass beamed. He gazed upwards as a seagull soared squawking above them, and chuckled to himself. 'That reminds me. Cap'n, I say, I say, I say: why does a seagull fly over the sea?'

Why does a seagull fly over the sea?

'I don't know,' Patch replied, treading carefully across the hot sand. 'Why *does* a seagull fly over the sea?'

'Because if it flew across the bay, it'd be a bagel,' Cutlass chortled. 'A *bay gull*, get it, matey?'

Patch laughed. Even Monty smirked.

If it flew across the bay, it'd be a bagel!

'Good one,' said Patch.

'Talking of bagels . . .' said Monty. 'I'm hungry. Is it banana time yet?'

'Any minute now,' Patch promised as they headed up the gangplank.

On board the *Golden Earring*, the rest of the crew were still rather subdued as they prepared to set sail.

'Never mind, Cap'n,' said Butch, trying to cheer him up. 'We might not have got the treasure this time, but at least we haven't been cursed. I'm not one to panic, but – between you

115

and me – I was a bit worried about that, you know . . .'

Captain Halibut gave a snort. 'Cursed? Codswallop,' he said . . . just as there was a huge **CRACK! FIZZ! BOOM!** from behind them.

They spun round just in time to see a freak bolt of lightning zapping the *Black Heart* . . . which immediately blew up the gunpowder barrels on deck. *KABLAM!* Captain Crunchbone's hat was blown clean off his head and went sailing through the air.

'Yikes!' he cried, leaping off the ship in alarm.

Within seconds, the *Black Heart* was ablaze. Smoke

116

billowed. Flames tore through the skull-and-crossbones flag, and the burning masts toppled into the sea.

SPLASH! SPLOSH! BADOOSH!

One by one, the crew followed their captain, diving into the sea.

Plop, plop, plop.

Then they were all swimming back to the island as fast as they could.

'Whoa!' cried Ginger, watching the scene from up in the crow's nest.

'So the treasure *was* cursed!' breathed Cannonball, his eyes bulging.

Captain Halibut gave a cough and fiddled with his beard. 'Which is why, of course, I *let* the *Black Heart* pirates have it,' he declared. 'Arrrr, didn't you realize that was my plan all along?'

The other pirates looked uncertain, as well they might.

'Umm . . .' said Ginger politely.

Just then,
Captain
Crunchbone's
hat, caught on
the breeze, flew
across to the
Golden Earring
where it landed
neatly on Patch's
head.

'Meow!' she cried in surprise.

'It's Captain Cat!' Butch
guffawed. 'Suits you, kitty!'

Captain Halibut snatched the hat off Patch's
head. 'There's only one captain around here,'
he said sternly, nailing it to the mast. 'But

this can be a lesson to any other pirates who think they can defeat the *Golden Earring* crew. Ahaarrr!'

'Ahaarrr!' the others cheered joyfully, even Patch, Cutlass and Monty.

'Let's get out of here,' Captain Halibut decided as ash started drifting across from the still-burning *Black Heart*. 'Hoist the mainsail! Anchor away! To our next amazing adventure . . . onward!'

Moments later, the *Golden Earring* was sailing away from the island and, as the sea breeze ruffled her fur, Patch felt as if she and her pirate pals had helped bring about a very lucky escape. In fact, it wasn't long at all before everything seemed to have returned to normal on board the ship.

Captain Halibut was putting his foot up and snoozing in his deckchair.

Cutlass was busily weaving Monty a crown out of feathers and shells and fish bones, as well as thinking up some excellent new jokes.

Monty was curled up in a coil of rope, nibbling one of the bananas Patch had pilfered for him and looking rather smug. 'I pushed Patch in the quicksand, I'm getting my very own crown, I've got three bananas all to myself AND I'm king of the ship,' he chortled. 'It's my lucky day!'

Ginger was up in the crow's nest, writing a postcard to her mum and dad to tell them all about her latest adventures.

Butch was at the ship's wheel, humming a

song to himself and making up some new words for it very quietly under his breath, so that he wouldn't get told off.

> 'Yo-ho-ho, and a bottle of rum,
> Captain Halibut's got a big bum.
> Our pirate crew is the bravest at sea,
> We're not scared of anything – 'specially not me!'

As for Patch the Captain Cat . . . well, after a sneaky spot of claw-sharpening on the mast, she had settled down in a warm pool of sunshine on deck for a cosy catnap. The ship was peaceful. Everything was calm. *Shush* . . . *shush* . . . sighed the sea against the sides of the ship and for once even the

screeching seagulls fell silent.

But just then . . . *BANG!* went the kitchen door, swinging open, and out came Cannonball. His apron was filthy, and there appeared to be a fish flapping in his pocket, but he looked *very* pleased with himself.

'Now I know we were all a bit disappointed about the treasure,' he announced, 'so I thought I'd make us some lovely grub to cheer everyone up. To start with, there's my legendary tentacle stew . . .'

Butch let out a whimper.

'And for afters I've made some yummy-scrummy jellyfish jelly!' Cannonball went on. 'Special treat!'

'B l e e u r g h ,' wailed Ginger.

Cannonball ignored them, beaming across at

Monty. 'As for my favourite little pal . . . there's an extra-big bowl for *you*. I insist. Come and get it!'

Patch couldn't help giggling at the look of pain on Monty's face that appeared with these words. 'Maybe you're not *quite* so lucky after all,' she teased him. Then, as the fish flung its way out of Cannonball's apron with a gigantic leap, Patch pounced on it with her two front paws, catching it neatly.

Oh YES! Sometimes, life as a pirate cat turns out to be quite purrfect, she thought with a grin.

THE END

Turn the page for an exclusive extract

from Captain Cat's next adventure . . .

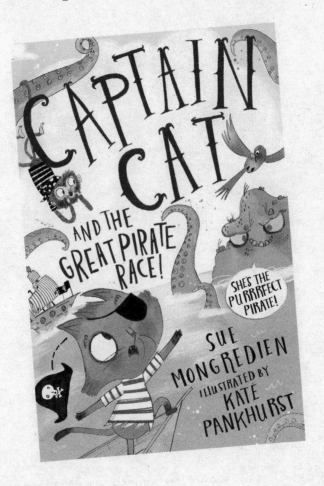

Chapter One

It was a breezy afternoon on board the *Golden Earring* and the crew was . . . well, the crew was nowhere to be seen, actually. The pirates had dropped anchor in Ingot Bay earlier that day and were now all enjoying some time on dry land, stretching their sea legs and loading supplies.

Captain Patch the cat was *supposed* to be guarding the ship to make sure they didn't have any unwanted visitors. As the **FIERCEST** pirate cat on all seven of the high seas, she had a terrifying s c o w l, a bone-chilling y o w l and a g r o w l that would make your hair stand on end.

But don't forget she was also a cat. A cat who really, REALLY liked fish. And the smell from the nearby docks was very hard to ignore.

M m m m . . . f i s h, she thought to herself, nostrils twitching dreamily at the pong.

It wouldn't hurt to slip away from the ship for a teeny, tiny minute, she decided, watching the fishing boats returning to the harbour with their hauls. You see, as well as being the fiercest pirate cat on all seven of the high seas, Patch also had highly effective tactics when it

2

came to begging for fish.

Sweet little *meow*? Tick.

Friendly rumbling *purr*? Tick.

Cute kitty face? Well . . . she did her best.

Most importantly, she was an expert when it came to winding around a person's legs. If she timed it perfectly, her victim would almost always stumble and trip, sending a nice fat fish plopping down on to the cobbles. YESSSS!

How could any cat resist? Patch trotted down the gangplank and got to work. Before long, she was having a whisker-lickingly good time. She polished off some plaice. She had a whole haddock. And she scoffed down some swordfish. Mmmmn!

Just then, Cutlass, the ship's parrot, landed

on a mooring post nearby. 'I say, I say, I say,' he squawked. 'Here's a joke for you, Cap'n!

Why did the baby octopus vanish?'

Patch picked her teeth with a fishbone and burped gently.

Why did the baby octopus vanish?

'Did I eat him?' she guessed.

'Nope – he was taken by **squidnappers**,' Cutlass chuckled. '*Squid*nappers. Geddit, matey?'

'You're squidding me,' Patch groaned. Cutlass might be her best pal,

He was taken by squidnappers

4

but sometimes his jokes were the *worst*. She gave the fishing boats a last loving look before she added, 'I suppose we should get back to the *Golden Earring* and guard the ship. This place is full of dodgy-looking pirates.'

'Talking of dodgy-looking pirates,' said Cutlass, 'here comes our crew. And what in Davy Jones's name has Captain Halibut got on his head?'

Patch and Cutlass stared as the *Golden Earring* crew strolled along the seafront together. They were a motley bunch, all right. Leading the way was Captain Halibut, who had clearly splashed out on a swashbuckling new pirate hat, decorated with very fancy gold thread.

'Ahoy there, handsome,' Patch heard him say

to his own reflection in a shop window.

Next was Cannonball, the ship's cook, who was hauling along a shiny new stew pot. 'Arrrr! This is just what I need for my seaweed casserole recipe,' he said, beaming. 'Special treat!'

Patch and Cutlass both groaned.

'He says "treat", I say "tummy upset",' sighed Cutlass.

Then there was Butch, tucking into an ice cream that was nearly as big as his head. He'd used his last pennies to buy a copy of *Pirate Comic* too.

'Win your own real treasure map,' he read aloud from the cover as he walked along. 'Cool!'

Patch raised a furry eyebrow at Cutlass. 'Has

he forgotten what happened last time?' she grumbled. After all, when the crew had found a different treasure map recently, there'd been *explosive* results!

Finally, there was Ginger, who'd just sent off a new postcard to her mum and dad. She'd also bought some sunglasses, which made her look *extremely* cool.

There was just one member of the crew missing.

'Where's Monty?' Cutlass asked, looking around.

Monty was the ship's monkey.

'He's at the funfair,' Patch said, pointing towards a huge, rattling rollercoaster that loomed over the sea. 'If you listen carefully, you can hear his screams on the breeze.'

'**A A A A R R R G G H H H H H !**

WHOOAAAAAAAA!' they heard just then.

'**EEEEEEEE! WOO-HOO-HOOOOO!**'

Patch and Cutlass grinned at one another . . .
but the smiles were wiped off their faces the
very next second when they heard a sneering
voice.

'**ARRRR!** Wallowing walruses, if it isn't
Captain Halibut himself!'

Patch's fur prickled immediately. Her tail
puffed up like a bottlebrush.

Cutlass's feathers trembled. 'Is that . . . ?' he
asked.

'Yep,' replied Patch as they turned and
eyed the tall pirate walking towards the *Golden*

Earring crew. It was Captain
Crunchbone, a **VILE** villain
and Halibut's sworn enemy. He
had a bushy red moustache, a
gold front tooth and a bone through his nostrils.
'What's *he* doing in Ingot Bay, I wonder?'

Being far too stupid to know animal
languages, the pirates only heard a meow and
couldn't understand what Patch was saying.
But the *Golden Earring* crew had noticed
Crunchbone too.

Butch gave a nervous whimper. 'Eep!'

Ginger peered anxiously over her new
sunglasses. 'Uh-oh.'

Cannonball whipped a rolling pin out of his
apron pocket and brandished it. 'Grrr!'

Then there was a cross-sounding *CLONK* as Captain Halibut stamped his wooden leg. 'Crunchbone, you horrible hagfish,' he said coldly. 'We meet again.' He tilted his snazzy new hat so that the sunshine twinkled brightly from the gold stitching, but if Crunchbone was impressed he didn't show it in the slightest.

'Halibut, you poxy poltroon,' replied Crunchbone, curling his lip. 'And there was me hoping you might have drowned by now and be just a heap of old bones at the bottom of the ocean.' He laughed meanly, showing blackened teeth. 'No such luck!'

'Ouch,' said Patch to Cutlass. 'Now *that's* harsh.'

Captain Halibut glared his most **fearsome**

glare at Crunchbone. 'If you've quite finished your **gibbering**,' he growled, 'I've got a ship to sail.'

'The *Golden Toilet*? Arrrr! Next you'll be telling me you're entering the Great Pirate Race with her tomorrow,' Crunchbone snorted. 'Ha ha ha ha!'

Captain Halibut's eyes blazed. He didn't take kindly to anyone insulting the *Golden Earring*, least of all his old enemy. 'How dare you?' he thundered. 'At least I've *got* a ship. As I recall, last time I saw you and your mangy crew, your rotten boat was on *fire*!'

Crunchbone gave a scornful laugh. 'That old

thing,' he sneered. 'Have you not seen what I'm captain of these days?' He pointed at the dock. 'Made an insurance claim, didn't I? Take a look at the *Dastardly Plunderer* over there, me hearties. She's mine, all mine.'

Everyone turned to follow Crunchbone's finger.

'Wowzers,' gulped Patch as she saw where he was pointing. The *Dastardly Plunderer* was a huge and handsome ship indeed, with a massive skull-and-crossbones flag, impressive shiny cannons and not one, not two, but THREE lookout points. Plus the mast looked *really* good for claw-sharpening.

'Cor,' sighed Ginger longingly. 'What a beauty.'

'Imagine the kitchen on that,' murmured

Cannonball with a dreamy expression.

'I bet the crew cabins have proper beds and everything,' said Butch, whose bunk was so tiny that he had to sleep with his feet sticking out at the end every night.

As for Captain Halibut, he just made a choking sound, too jealous to even speak.

Patch glanced back over at the *Golden Earring* with its tatty sails, its tangled rigging and shabby cabins and felt a tingle of envy herself. Next to the *Dastardly Plunderer*, it looked a complete **wreck.**

Captain Crunchbone smirked a horrible, gloaty smirk. 'Good, eh? I reckon there'll only be one winner of the Great Pirate Race tomorrow,' he said. 'And something tells me it won't be *you*, old Halibobs.'

Patch had never heard of the Great Pirate Race and she was pretty sure Captain Halibut hadn't either – which was why she was surprised when he snapped, 'Oh, *really?* We'll just see about that. Fifty gold coins says *we'll* win it, thank you very much! Arrrr!'

Captain Crunchbone hooted with laughter and slapped his raggedy-trousered thigh. 'Ha ha! In your dreams, sunshine.'

Meanwhile, the rest of the *Golden Earring* crew were gazing at one another in alarm.

'Great Pirate Race?' whispered Ginger. 'Do you have to be great to enter it, do you think, or can any old pirate take part?'

Butch's enormous knees were knocking together. 'I don't like the sound of it,' he muttered anxiously. 'I've got a bad feeling about this race. It might be *dangerous*!'

'I'd better stock up on grub,' Cannonball fretted. 'Maybe some jellyfish fritters will help the captain run faster.'

'Run faster?' repeated Captain Crunchbone, overhearing. He threw back his head and laughed so hard the bone through his nostrils waggled. *'Run faster?* Bellowing barnacles, Halibut, you've got a crew of dimwits here and no mistake! The Great Pirate Race is a *sailing* race, not a running race – from Ingot Bay to Hammerhead Island. Ha! I'll see you at the finish line . . . when you arrive there in last place. As long as your crummy old ship doesn't sink on the way!'

And, with that, he barged past Halibut, still sniggering, and disappeared into the Piratical Emporium of Bloodthirsty Bargains.

'That flame-haired flounder,' growled Captain Halibut. 'That rotten-toothed rogue. He'll be laughing on the other side of his ugly face when we romp over the finish line in first place and seize the prize. Just you wait!'

TO BE
CONTINUED . . .

About the author

Sue Mongredien has had over one hundred children's books published, including the Oliver Moon and Secret Mermaid series' for Usborne, and the Prince Jake books for Orchard. She is also one of the authors behind the internationally bestselling Rainbow Magic series, as Daisy Meadows. She lives in Bath with her husband and their three children. *Captain Cat and the Treasure Map* is the first in the Captain Cat series.

About the illustrator

Kate Pankhurst lives in Leeds with her family and her spotty dog, Olive. She has a studio based in an old spinning mill where she writes and illustrates children's books. Recent projects have included the bestselling Fantastically Great Women series and the Mariella Mystery Investigates series. Kate is distantly related to the suffragette Emmeline Pankhurst, something that has been an influence on the type of books she enjoys creating for children.